Today on Election Day

Catherine Stier   Illustrated by David Leonard

Albert Whitman & Company, Chicago, Illinois

Also by Catherine Stier:
If I Were President
If I Ran for President

To our country's future voters, who will one day shape our nation by casting their ballots; and to Andrew, who will vote for his first time on this Election Day.—C.S.

For my girls who elected me "King David."—D.L.

Library of Congress Cataloging-in-Publication Data

Stier, Catherine.
Today on election day / Catherine Stier ; illustrated by David Leonard.
p. cm.
ISBN 978-0-8075-8008-0 (hardcover)
1. Elections—United States—History—Juvenile literature. 2. Election Day—History—Juvenile literature. I. Leonard, David, 1979- ill. II. Title.
JK1978.S846 2012 324.60973—dc23 2011035248

The design is by Carol Gildar.

For more information about Albert Whitman,
Please visit our Web site at www.albertwhitman.com.

Election Day truly is a special day in the United States.

On Election Day, we vote to choose who will be the leaders of our state and country, and perhaps our city or town, too.

Elections for local offices may be held at different times of the year. However, in 1845, Congress set a national Election Day for electing the president, vice president, and members of the US Congress. These elections are always in November, on the first Tuesday following the first Monday of the month. Presidential elections are held in an even-numbered year, on this day, every four years.

In some years voters can choose a governor, the leader of their state. Some will choose members of Congress—senators or members of the House of Representatives. They may vote for city or county officers, or judges. They may also consider proposals for new rules or laws for their state, city, or county. US citizens are not required to vote, but it is an important right and responsibility. In most cases, as long as a person is a United States citizen, is at least eighteen years old, follows voter registration rules, and has not committed a serious crime, he or she may vote. How many years until you are eighteen? That's when you can join the citizens who shape the country—and the future—by voting!

The **Fifteenth Amendment** (1870) states that people of any race or color can vote (however, it was the Voting Rights Act of 1965 that finally ensured that these rights were protected). The **Nineteenth Amendment** (1920) granted women the right to vote.

Finally, the **Twenty-Sixth Amendment** (1971) set the minimum age for voting in all states at eighteen.

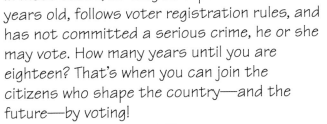

This is no ordinary day.

A star marks this date on the class calendar. Through the window, we see grown-ups coming and going to our school. Something important is happening today right here in our town, and all over the USA. Something so big, it will shape the future. It will go down in history.

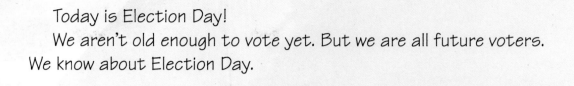

Today is Election Day!
 We aren't old enough to vote yet. But we are all future voters.
We know about Election Day.

Today on Election Day, the excitement started early!
Television newscasters reported on the election while I munched
my breakfast. On the way to my school safety patrol job,
I passed signs with the names and pictures of candidates.
Candidates are the people running for office.

Our crossing guard stayed extra-busy this morning! She stopped traffic for us kids as usual, but also for construction workers, restaurant servers, and a pilot. I saw people in suits, running clothes, and uniforms. They drove, walked, jogged, pedaled bikes, steered a wheelchair, and pushed strollers, all on their way to our school.

That's because today our school gym is set up as a polling place—a place where people vote!

In some towns, people vote at a town hall, the library, or even the firehouse.

Our country is set up as a democracy. That's a system of governing that allows citizens to choose their own leaders.

It's pretty amazing to know that is what's happening in our school today!

Today on Election Day, voters will choose the next president of the United States. I'm our class president, and it's an important and very busy job. Imagine being leader of a whole country!

Candidates for president usually come from two main political parties, the Democratic Party and the Republican Party. You might see each party's symbol—a donkey for the Democrats and an elephant for Republicans—on signs, bumpers stickers, or in political cartoons. Sometimes candidates from other political parties are "on the ballot." That means they are running for office, too.

Whether they are running for president or for a local office, candidates and their supporters will run a campaign. Campaigns are designed to try to gain popularity—and votes—for the candidate. Campaigns also give candidates a chance to share their ideas with the American people.

Campaigns can be expensive! Candidates and their supporters may create signs and commercials, host rallies, and plan appearances to meet the voters.

Choosing the president is a big decision, but it's not the only decision voters might make on Election Day.

In some states, voters will choose a governor, the leader of their state. Some will choose members of Congress—senators or members of the House of Representatives.

So much will be decided today!

Today on Election Day, men and women all over the country will cast their ballots—which means they will vote. But women weren't always allowed to vote. And long ago, other citizens were kept from voting, too. I know, because I wrote a report for our class Web site.

At one time in our country, white men who were rich enough to own property were often the only people allowed to vote.

Through the years, people protested against these voting rules.

In the late 1800s, Elizabeth Cady Stanton, Susan B. Anthony, and others called for women's voting rights.

In the mid-1900s, Dr. Martin Luther King, Jr. worked to protect African-Americans' right to vote.

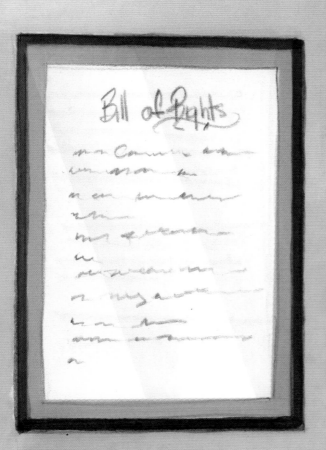

The efforts of these and other citizens eventually led to new laws as well as changes, called amendments, to the US Constitution.

Today, people are allowed to vote no matter their gender, race, or how much money or property they have.

Today on Election Day, my big brother Jake will vote for the first time. He turned eighteen this summer and he registered to vote. He takes his responsibility as a voter seriously! Jake read about the candidates in the newspapers and on Web sites. He talked about the election with his friends.

One night, he watched a presidential debate on television. During the debate, a moderator asked candidates questions. Jake said watching the debate helped him decide which candidate's ideas he liked best.

Jake also learned about other issues on the ballot. He is especially interested in proposals about the environment and education.

And look, there's Jake zooming past. He is going to take me with him when he goes to vote.

Today on Election Day, my grandpa picks me up after school. We head to the polling place at the gym. Now I can see for myself how voting works!

Inside the gym, I see the fitness posters and the big basket of playground balls. There are also rows of stands with curtains—voting booths!

We line up for our turn. A poll worker checks a voter registration list and my grandpa's identification. She smiles and points out an open voting booth.

Nobody knows who you vote for unless you tell them, because in the United States we have what is known as a secret ballot.

My grandpa has been a voter for a long time. He says he remembers when he used to vote by pushing down levers on a voting machine. He also recalls punching a card and even marking a paper ballot. In some places in our country, people still vote in those ways. Today my grandpa will cast his vote by touching a computer screen.

When Grandpa touches a box next to his choice of candidate,
a checkmark appears. How cool is that?

After my grandpa is finished voting, he touches the screen once more so his votes will be recorded. His votes will be tallied—that means counted up—with all the other votes cast by millions of United States citizens today.

As we leave, an election volunteer gives Grandpa a "VOTED TODAY" sticker.

He proudly puts that sticker on his jacket.

Today on Election Day, my Aunt Julia hopes to be elected to our city council. As a councilwoman, Aunt Julia will work with the mayor and other council members to improve our town. She'll help make important decisions, like whether the new town park should have a soccer field or a playground.

I helped Aunt Julia with her campaign. I even helped design her signs.

I think she will make a great councilwoman. We find out tonight
if voters in our town agree!

My parents and I gather with Aunt Julia and her supporters.
Everyone is excited.

All evening, we watch a big TV screen as the newscasters report
on the election results.

Suddenly, my mother pats me awake. "Good news!" she says. "Aunt Julia just found out she's been elected!"

My eyes pop open.

"Hooray!" I hear from Aunt Julia's supporters.

On the television screen, the newscasters have announced the outcome of the presidential election, too. I watch the winners and their families wave to a huge, cheering crowd.

I jump up and cheer, too—for Aunt Julia, for our democracy,
and for the United States of America!
And that's what happened today on Election Day!